DREAMLAND

EASY DRAW

...STEP BY STEP

BY
ANI DAS
M.F.A.

Published by
DREAMLAND PUBLICATIONS
J-128, KIRTI NAGAR, NEW DELHI-110 015, INDIA
PHONE : +91-11-2510 6050, 2543 5657
E-mail : dreamland@vsnl.com
Shop online at www.dreamlandpublications.com
Like us on www.facebook.com/DreamlandPublications

SHAPES WE HAVE LEARNT.

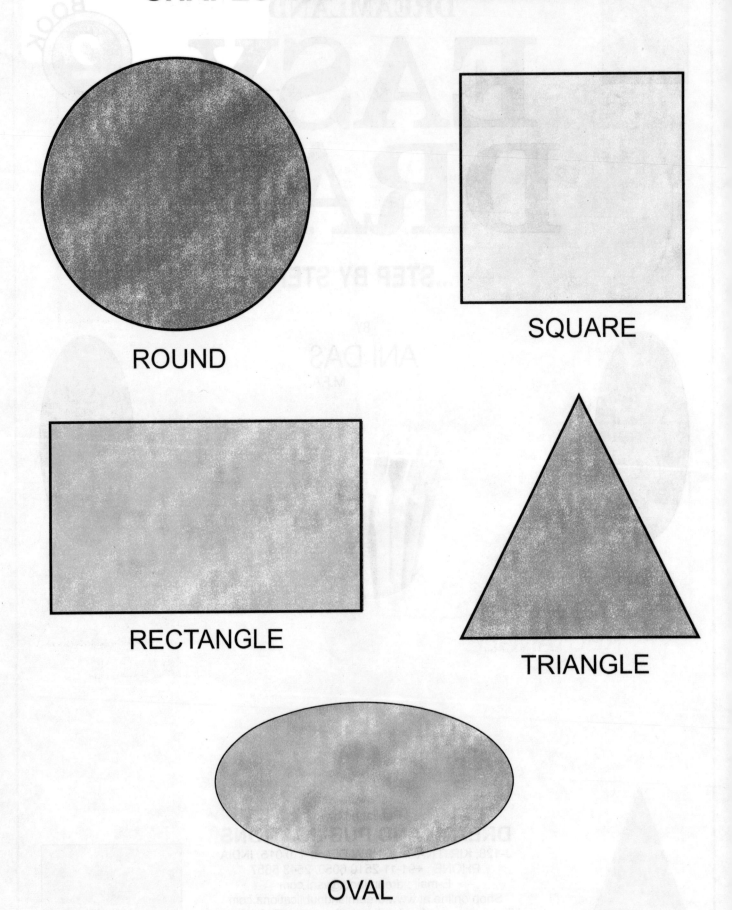

ROUND

SQUARE

RECTANGLE

TRIANGLE

OVAL

COLOUR THESE SHAPES.

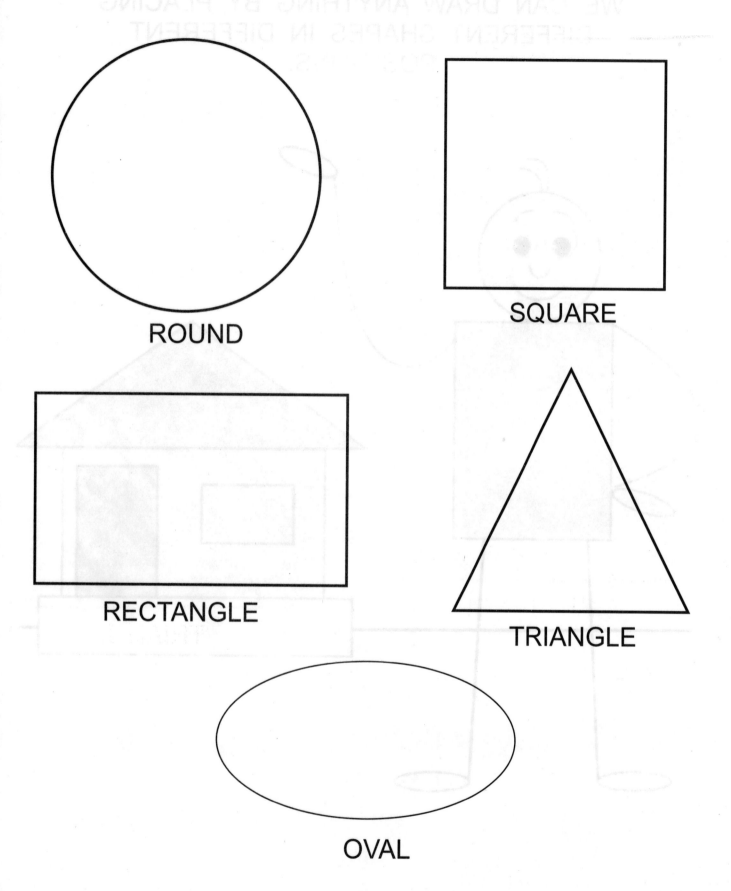

ROUND

SQUARE

RECTANGLE

TRIANGLE

OVAL

PLAY WITH SHAPES.

WE CAN DRAW ANYTHING BY PLACING DIFFERENT SHAPES IN DIFFERENT POSITIONS.

WE CAN DRAW THE SUN
USING ROUND AND TRIANGULAR SHAPES.

NOW TRY TO DRAW THE SUN YOURSELF
AND COLOUR IT SIMILARLY.

WE CAN DRAW A FLOWER
USING ROUND AND OVAL SHAPES.

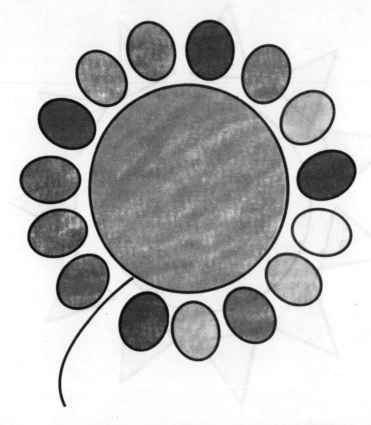

NOW TRY TO DRAW
THE FLOWER AND COLOUR IT SIMILARLY.

WE CAN DRAW A FRUIT
USING A ROUND AND AN OVAL SHAPE.

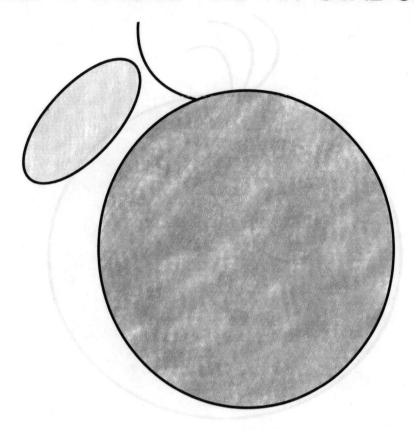

NOW TRY TO DRAW THE FRUIT
YOURSELF AND COLOUR IT SIMILARLY.

WE CAN DRAW A FACE USING
ROUND SHAPES AND CURVED SHAPES.

NOW TRY TO DRAW THE FACE
YOURSELF AND COLOUR IT SIMILARLY.

8

WE CAN DRAW A TREE USING
OVAL AND TRIANGULAR SHAPES.

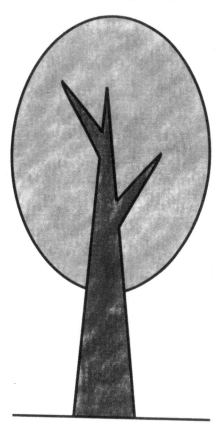

NOW TRY TO DRAW
THE TREE AND COLOUR IT SIMILARLY.

WE CAN DRAW A WINDOW USING SQUARE SHAPES.

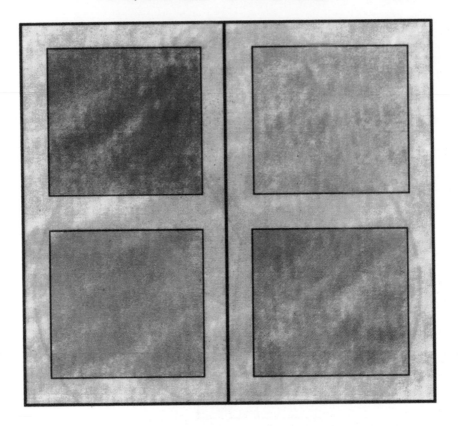

NOW TRY TO DRAW
THE WINDOW AND COLOUR IT SIMILARLY.

WE CAN DRAW A KITE USING
A SQUARE AND A TRIANGULAR SHAPE.

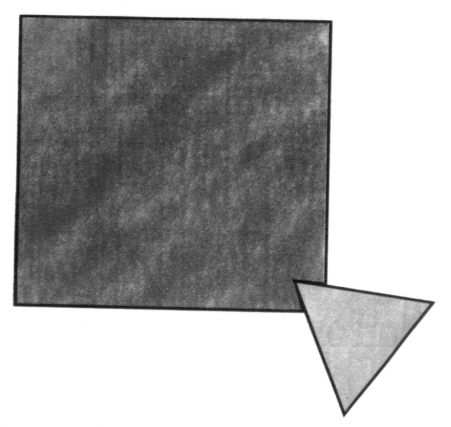

NOW TRY TO DRAW
THE KITE AND COLOUR IT SIMILARLY.

WE CAN DRAW A DOOR
USING RECTANGULAR SHAPES.

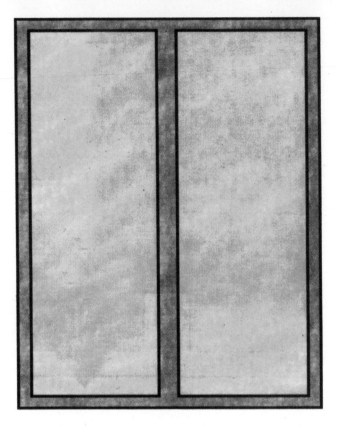

NOW TRY TO DRAW
THE DOOR AND COLOUR IT SIMILARLY.

WE CAN DRAW A STAR
USING TRIANGULAR SHAPES.

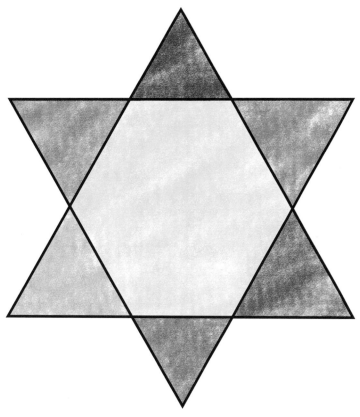

NOW TRY TO DRAW
THE STAR AND COLOUR IT SIMILARLY.

WE CAN DRAW A CHRISTMAS TREE USING
TRIANGULAR SHAPES AND STRAIGHT LINES.

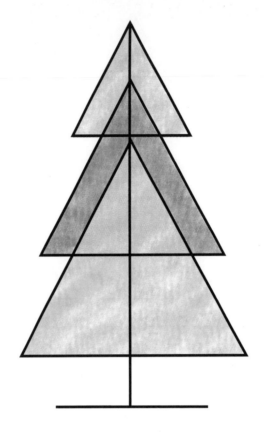

NOW TRY TO DRAW THE CHRISTMAS
TREE AND COLOUR IT SIMILARLY.

WE CAN DRAW A HUT AND A HOUSE
USING SQUARE, RECTANGULAR AND
TRIANGULAR SHAPES.

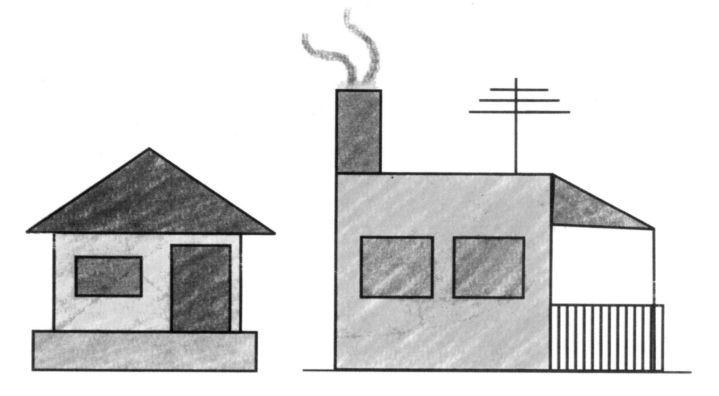

NOW TRY TO DRAW THE HUT AND THE
HOUSE AND COLOUR THEM SIMILARLY.

WE CAN DRAW A FISH USING ROUND, OVAL AND TRIANGULAR SHAPES.

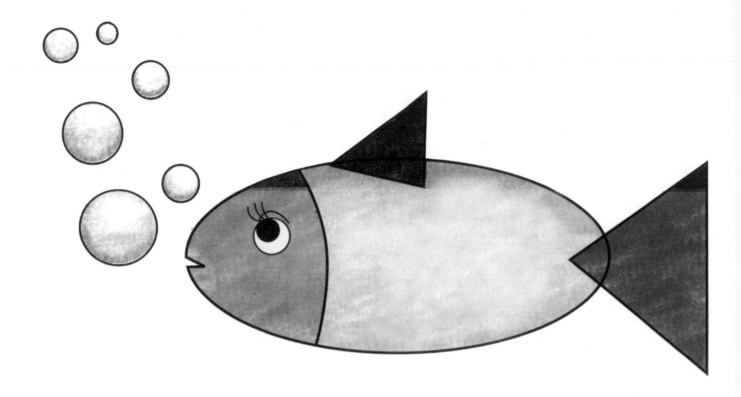

NOW TRY TO DRAW THE FISH AND COLOUR IT SIMILARLY.

WE CAN DRAW A BIRD USING ROUND,
OVAL AND TRIANGULAR SHAPES.

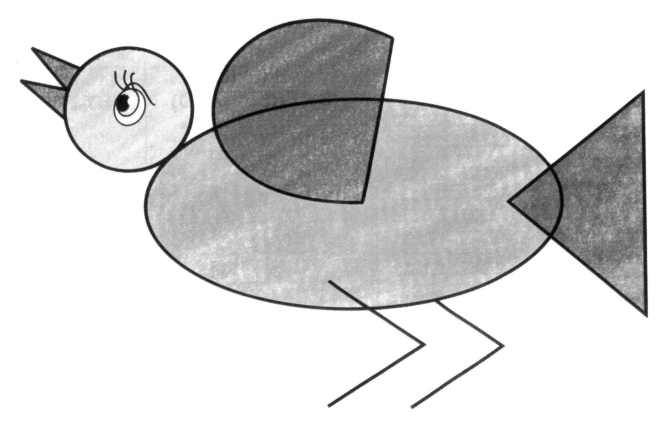

NOW TRY TO DRAW THE BIRD
AND COLOUR IT SIMILARLY.

FUN WITH LINES
LET'S DO SOME SIMPLE EXERCISES IN LINES.

TRY IT HERE.
(BY FREE HAND)

TRY IT HERE.
(BY FREE HAND)

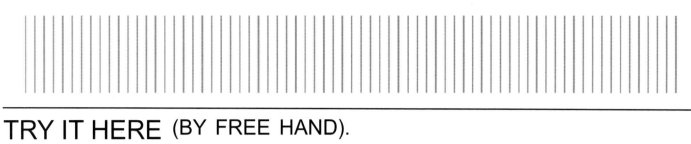

TRY IT HERE (BY FREE HAND).

TRY IT HERE (BY FREE HAND).

TRY IT HERE (BY FREE HAND).

TRY IT HERE (BY FREE HAND).

TRY IT HERE (BY FREE HAND).

TRY IT HERE (BY FREE HAND).

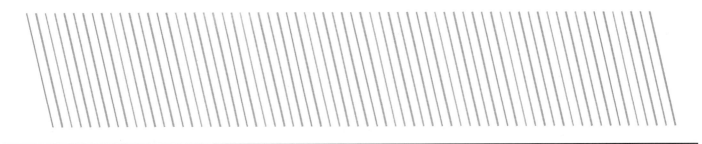

TRY IT HERE (BY FREE HAND).

TRY IT HERE (BY FREE HAND).

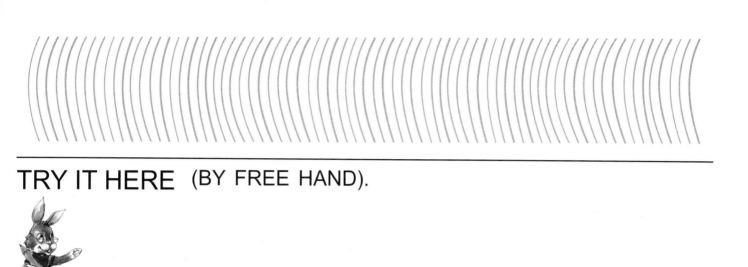

TRY IT HERE (BY FREE HAND).

TRY IT HERE (BY FREE HAND).

TRY IT HERE (BY FREE HAND).

TRY IT HERE (BY FREE HAND).

	TRY IT HERE. (BY FREE HAND)	**TRY IT HERE.** (BY FREE HAND)	**TRY IT HERE.** (BY FREE HAND)
	TRY IT HERE. (BY FREE HAND)	**TRY IT HERE.** (BY FREE HAND)	**TRY IT HERE.** (BY FREE HAND)

TRY IT HERE (BY FREE HAND).

TRY IT HERE (BY FREE HAND).

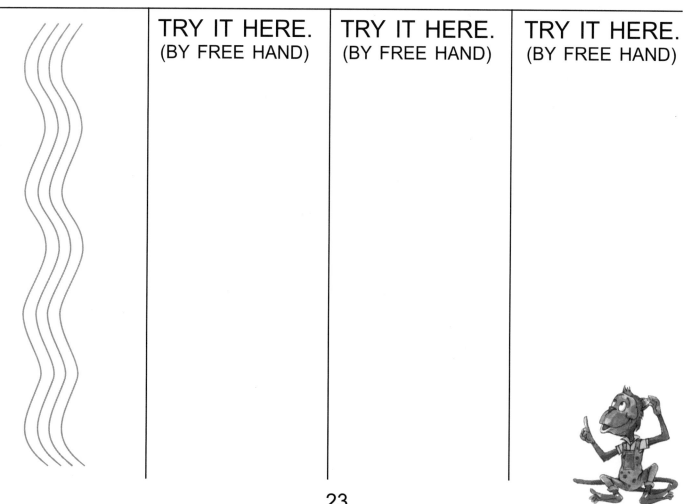

	TRY IT HERE. (BY FREE HAND)	TRY IT HERE. (BY FREE HAND)	TRY IT HERE. (BY FREE HAND)

NOW WE CAN DRAW SOME SIMPLE THINGS USING CURVED LINES.

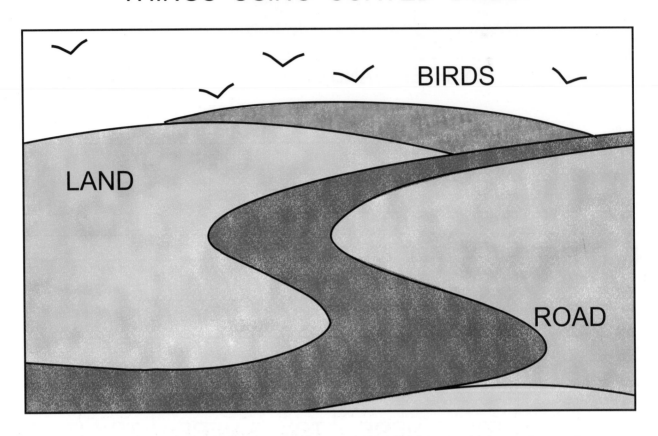

TRY TO DRAW THE THINGS YOURSELF
AND COLOUR THEM SIMILARLY.

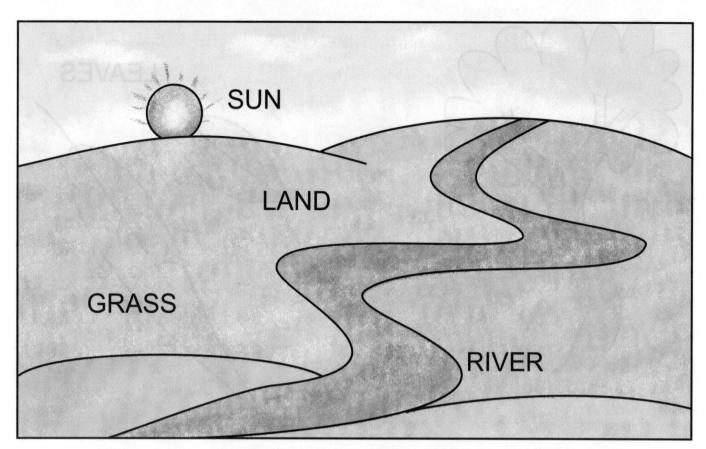

SUN

LAND

GRASS

RIVER

TRY TO DRAW THE THINGS YOURSELF
AND COLOUR THEM SIMILARLY.

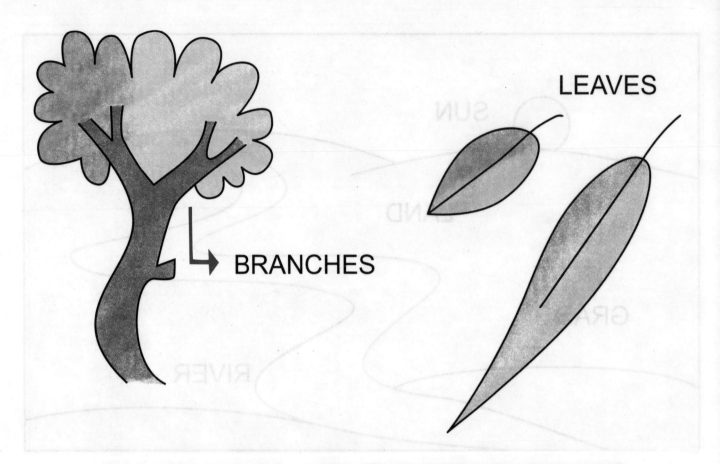

LEAVES

BRANCHES

TRY TO DRAW LEAVES AND BRANCHES
AND COLOUR THEM SIMILARLY.

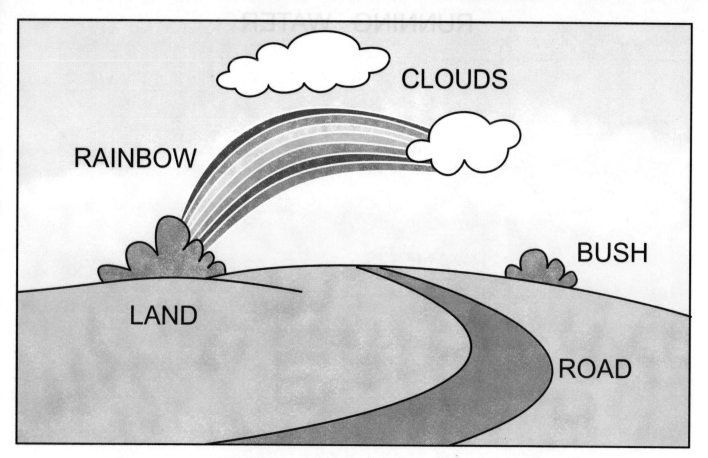

TRY TO DRAW THE THINGS YOURSELF
AND COLOUR THEM SIMILARLY.

RUNNING WATER

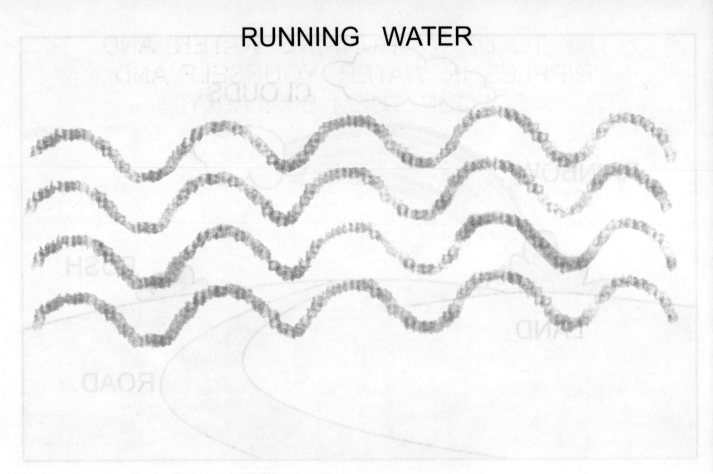

RIPPLES IN WATER

TRY TO DRAW 'RUNNING WATER' AND 'RIPPLES IN WATER' YOURSELF AND COLOUR THEM SIMILARLY.

STANDING WATER

SEA WATER

TRY TO DRAW 'STANDING WATER' AND 'SEA WATER' YOURSELF AND COLOUR THEM SIMILARLY.

EXERCISE

TRY TO DRAW ANYTHING YOU SEE
AROUND YOU, WITH THE HELP OF
DIFFERENT SHAPES AND LINES
YOU HAVE LEARNT.